For all at Auchterhouse Primary School
J.D.

First published 1999 by Macmillan Children's Books
This edition published 2019 by Macmillan Children's Books
an imprint of Pan Macmillan
20 New Wharf Road, London N1 9RR
Associated companies throughout the world
www.panmacmillan.com

ISBN 978-1-5098-9413-0

Photography: pages 30–31 (except black-and-white photo), Steve Ullathorne;
page 33, Eliz Hüseyin; page 35, *The Gruffalo* cast photo © Tall Stories;
page 35, The Gruffalo River Ride Adventure - photography Mikael Buck;
page 35, photos from *The Gruffalo* film © Orange Eyes Ltd 2009
Courtesy of Magic Light Pictures Ltd.

1 3 5 7 9 8 6 4 2

A CIP catalogue record for this book is available from the British Library.

Printed in China

WRITTEN BY
JULIA DONALDSON

ILLUSTRATED BY
AXEL SCHEFFLER

THE GRUFFALO

MACMILLAN CHILDREN'S BOOKS

A mouse took a stroll through the deep dark wood.
A fox saw the mouse and the mouse looked good.
"Where are you going to, little brown mouse?
Come and have lunch in my underground house."
"It's terribly kind of you, Fox, but no —
I'm going to have lunch with a gruffalo."

"A gruffalo? What's a gruffalo?"
"A gruffalo! Why, didn't you know?

"He has terrible tusks,   and terrible claws,

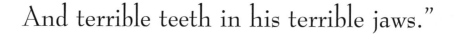

And terrible teeth in his terrible jaws."

"*Where are you meeting him?*"
"Here, by these rocks,
And his favourite food is roasted fox."

"Roasted fox! I'm off!" Fox said.
"Goodbye, little mouse," and away he sped.

"Silly old Fox! Doesn't he know,
There's no such thing as a gruffalo?"

On went the mouse through the deep dark wood.
An owl saw the mouse and the mouse looked good.
*"Where are you going to, little brown mouse?
Come and have tea in my treetop house."*
"It's frightfully nice of you, Owl, but no —
I'm going to have tea with a gruffalo."

"A gruffalo? What's a gruffalo?"
"A gruffalo! Why, didn't you know?

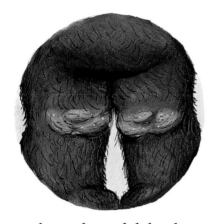 

"He has knobbly knees, and turned-out toes,

And a poisonous wart at the end of his nose."

"*Where are you meeting him?*"
"Here, by this stream,
And his favourite food is owl ice cream."

"Owl ice cream? Toowhit toowhoo!
Goodbye, little mouse," and away Owl flew.

"Silly old Owl! Doesn't he know,
There's no such thing as a gruffalo?"

On went the mouse through the deep dark wood.
A snake saw the mouse and the mouse looked good.
"*Where are you going to, little brown mouse?*
Come for a feast in my logpile house."
"It's wonderfully good of you, Snake, but no —
I'm having a feast with a gruffalo."

"*A gruffalo? What's a gruffalo?*"
"A gruffalo! Why, didn't you know?

"His eyes are orange,   his tongue is black;

He has purple prickles all over his back."

"*Where are you meeting him?*"
"Here, by this lake,
And his favourite food is scrambled snake."

"Scrambled snake! It's time I hid!
Goodbye, little mouse," and away Snake slid.

"Silly old Snake! Doesn't he know,
There's no such thing as a gruffal . . .

. . . Oh!"

But who is this creature with terrible claws
And terrible teeth in his terrible jaws?
He has knobbly knees and turned-out toes
And a poisonous wart at the end of his nose.
His eyes are orange, his tongue is black;
He has purple prickles all over his back.

"Oh help! Oh no!
It's a gruffalo!"

"My favourite food!" the Gruffalo said.
"You'll taste good on a slice of bread!"

"Good?" said the mouse. "Don't call me good!
I'm the scariest creature in this wood.
Just walk behind me and soon you'll see,
Everyone is afraid of me."

"*All right,*" said the Gruffalo, bursting with laughter.
"*You go ahead and I'll follow after.*"

They walked and walked till the Gruffalo said,
"*I hear a hiss in the leaves ahead.*"

"It's Snake," said the mouse. "Why, Snake, hello!"
Snake took one look at the Gruffalo.
"*Oh crumbs!*" he said, "*Goodbye, little mouse,*"
And off he slid to his logpile house.

"You see?" said the mouse. "I told you so."
"*Amazing!*" said the Gruffalo.

They walked some more till the Gruffalo said,
"*I hear a hoot in the trees ahead.*"

"It's Owl," said the mouse. "Why, Owl, hello!"
Owl took one look at the Gruffalo.
"*Oh dear!*" he said, "*Goodbye, little mouse,*"
And off he flew to his treetop house.

"You see?" said the mouse. "I told you so."
"Astounding!" said the Gruffalo.

They walked some more till the Gruffalo said,
"I can hear feet on the path ahead."

"It's Fox," said the mouse. "Why, Fox, hello!"
Fox took one look at the Gruffalo.
"*Oh help!*" he said, "*Goodbye, little mouse,*"
And off he ran to his underground house.

"Well, Gruffalo," said the mouse. "You see?
Everyone is afraid of me!
But now my tummy's beginning to rumble.
My favourite food is — gruffalo crumble!"

"*Gruffalo crumble!*" the Gruffalo said,
And quick as the wind he turned and fled.

All was quiet in the deep dark wood.
The mouse found a nut and the nut was good.

Do you know the Gruffalo?

See if you can answer these questions.

You can find the answers in the story.

What does the Gruffalo have at the end of his nose?

What colour are the Gruffalo's eyes?

What has the Gruffalo got all over his back?

Who invites the mouse for tea in a treetop house?

Who invites the mouse for a feast in a logpile house?

Which animal does the mouse say the Gruffalo likes roasted?

Which animal does the mouse say the Gruffalo likes scrambled?

How does the Gruffalo think the mouse will taste good?

Who says his favourite food is gruffalo crumble?

What does the mouse eat at the end of the story?

The Gruffalo Song

He has terrible tusks and terrible claws

*(Curl both index fingers and put them up to your teeth like tusks.
Then put your fingers out like claws.)*

and terrible teeth in his terrible jaws.

(Show your teeth.)

He's the Gruffalo, Gruffalo, Gruffalo.
He's the Gruffalo.

(Make claws with your fingers and dance from foot to foot.)

He has knobbly knees and turned-out toes

(Rub your knees and stand with toes pointing out.)

and a poisonous wart at the end of his nose.

(Point to your nose.)

He's the Gruffalo, Gruffalo, Gruffalo.
He's the Gruffalo.

(Make claws with your fingers and dance from foot to foot.)

His eyes are orange. His tongue is black.

(Point to your eyes and stick out your tongue.)

He has purple prickles all over his back.

(Scratch your back.)

He's the Gruffalo, Gruffalo, Gruffalo.
He's the Gruffalo, Gruffalo, Gruffalo.
He's the Grr . . . rr . . . rr . . . rr . . . ruffalo.

(Make claws with your fingers and dance from foot to foot.)

HE'S THE GRUFFALO!

Watch Julia sing the song with Makaton actions on the Gruffalo website: www.gruffalo.com/songs

Grrrrrowl like a gruffalo when you say 'Grrr . . . rr . . . rr . . . rr . . . ruffalo'!

Shout the last line as loud as you can!

A Gruffalo!
Why, didn't you know?

The Gruffalo began when I read an old Chinese tale about a clever girl who tricks a hungry tiger. What a good idea for a picture book, I thought. But not many words rhyme with 'tiger'! (Can you think of any?)

So I thought really hard and came up with the word 'gruffalo' to rhyme with 'know' (as in "Silly old Fox, doesn't he know. . ."). And that's how I created the character of the Gruffalo!

I nearly gave up writing it halfway through. I just couldn't get the rhymes to work. But my son Alastair (who was about 14 at the time) said, "Don't give up, Mum. I think it's good!" So I managed to finish the book.

When I wrote the story, I imagined the Gruffalo to be a sort of alien creature. Then I saw Axel's drawing and I thought, well, of course that's what he looks like!

When we were little, my sister Mary and I loved to put on shows. In this picture, I'm the bucket and Mary is the spade.

Now, I've performed *The Gruffalo* all over the world. Mary still performs with me, and so does my husband, Malcolm. When we act out the story, I'm the mouse, Mary is the owl and Malcolm is the fox with his smart red hat.

Here I am as the mouse in the deep dark wood. I'm telling the snake that I don't want to join him for a feast in his logpile house. I think he might want to make *me* the feast!

Julia Donaldson

 # Drawing the Gruffalo

I first met the Gruffalo back in 1998 when Julia sent me a letter with the story typed out on a few sheets of paper.

The word 'gruffalo' made me think of a 'buffalo', so first of all I drew him with horns and a tail and walking on all fours. Then I decided he might look better standing up.

And he did look better. But my editor thought that he was too scary! So I changed him a bit.

The animals changed from my first sketches too. At first, I thought they should wear clothes, but what kind of clothes would a snake wear? This was a tricky problem. Luckily, Julia didn't think clothes were necessary.

Mouse

To draw the Gruffalo, first I make a pencil sketch. Then I draw over the pencil outline with black ink using a dip pen. I keep dipping the pen into the inkpot!

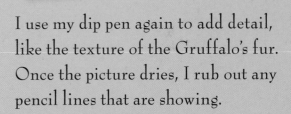

I use my dip pen again to add detail, like the texture of the Gruffalo's fur. Once the picture dries, I rub out any pencil lines that are showing.

Next, I colour the picture with watercolours. I used up all my browns and greens for *The Gruffalo* book.

Here are the Gruffalo and the mouse!

The World of the Gruffalo

Can you guess how many copies of *The Gruffalo* have been sold around the world? More than 13.5 million. If you piled them all up, they would be 10 times taller than Mount Everest, the tallest mountain in the world!

You can read *The Gruffalo* in 76 different languages. He has different names in different languages, too.

Here are just a few of them . . .

Το Γκρούφαλο
Greek

Mörkyli
Finnish

Yayazula
Turkish

גְּרוּפוֹתִי
Hebrew

Gruffalon
Swedish

古飛樂
Mandarin

グラファロ
もりでいちばん
つよいのは?
Japanese

Die Goorgomgaai
Afrikaans

A Spasso col Mostro
Italian

Y Gryffalo
Welsh

Bubulis un Bubulēns
Latvian

Der Grüffelo
German

الغرفول
Arabic

ГРУФФАЛО
Russian

El Grúfalo
Spanish

Greppikló
Icelandic

O Grufalão
Portuguese

Grøfler
Danish

Out and About

Oh help! Oh no! It's a gruffalo! And he isn't only in the pages of a book.
You might also see him . . .

. . . on the screen.

. . . in the theatre.

. . . in a theme park.

Did you know *The Gruffalo*
story has been made into an
award-winning film?

There's even a Gruffalo River
Ride Adventure at Chessington
World of Adventures Resort.

Astounding!

There's a stage show too. Children
have enjoyed seeing *The Gruffalo*
acted out for over 15 years.

Amazing!

Here he is in Canada admiring the
Toronto skyline.

The Gruffalo
sometimes appears
at very special
shows around
the world . . .

Maybe you'll
meet him?

And here he is in Sydney, Australia.
G'day, Gruffalo!

Gruffalo play scene

Setting up

The deep dark wood play scene is inside the jacket of your book. To play with it, first stand the play scene up on a flat surface, such as a table or floor. Carefully press out the Gruffalo, Mouse, Fox, Owl and Snake characters. You can find them at the back of this book. Fold back the base at the bottom of each character so they can stand up on their own. Now you're ready to play!

When you have finished playing, keep your press-out characters in an envelope or a box so they don't get lost.

Move your characters around in front of the deep dark wood play scene. Maybe the characters can chase each other, or hide, or give each other a fright! What else can they do? You could even put on a show . . .

Can you spot Fox's underground house, Owl's treetop house and Snake's logpile house in the deep dark wood?

Put on a Gruffalo show

You could put on a *Gruffalo* show for your family. First, look at the pictures in the story to help you remember what happens. Try telling the story yourself, using the characters. Then have fun practising the show before putting it on for an audience.

How about making funny voices for the characters? You might try making them all sound different. Mouse's voice might be squeaky. Owl hoots and Snake hisses. What do you think Fox sounds like? Of course you'll need a very deep grrrrrrrrrrowl for the Gruffalo!

Perhaps your friends would like to put on the show with you. Decide who will play which character. (But don't squabble about it or the Gruffalo might eat you!)

You could ask a grown-up to read the story out loud while you put on the show with the characters in the play scene.

Sing the song

How about singing The Gruffalo Song for your audience? You can sing it as part of your show. It would be a great way to finish your performance and perhaps your audience will want to sing along too!

Posters

Posters are a fantastic way to tell people about your puppet show. Make sure to put on the poster when and where your show is taking place.

THE GRUFFALO PLAY
WHERE? IN THE LIVING ROOM
WHEN? 4 PM

Tickets

You could make tickets for your audience. Give a ticket to everyone who is coming to your show, and then check their tickets when your audience arrives.

Programmes

Make programmes to give your audience, too. Fold a piece of paper in half like a little booklet. Put THE GRUFFALO on the front and decorate it. Inside, make a list of the characters and the names of all the people who are performing in your show.

Make up your own stories

Can you make up more stories with your play scene? What would happen if Mouse did have lunch with Fox, tea with Owl and a feast with Snake? What might happen if Mouse and the Gruffalo met again? Have fun thinking up new ideas and putting on lots of different shows!